Last Chance
for Magic

by RUTH CHEW
Illustrated by the author

Cover illustration by Rudy Nappi

A
LITTLE APPLE
PAPERBACK

SCHOLASTIC INC.
New York Toronto London Auckland Sydney

ISBN 0-590-60210-1

12 11 10 9 8 7 6 5 4 3 2 1   6 7 8 9/9 0 1/0

Printed in the U.S.A.   40

First Scholastic printing, April 1996

For Betty Bartelt Howard

1

"Out of the way, everybody!" Mr. Robertson yelled. "This fence is coming down!"

Terry and her brother, Max, jumped back. Their mother was behind them. She pulled both of them even farther from the tall old fence.

The Robertsons had moved into the house last week. Like many houses in Brooklyn, this one was joined in a row with others. The houses looked alike, and each had a backyard with a fence around it.

There was a row of the same kind of houses on the other side of the block.

Yesterday, when their father left the stepladder in the front yard, Max and

Terry took turns climbing it to look over the back fence.

They saw there was a vacant lot between the two rows of houses. All sorts of trees and bushes crowded next to each other in the lot. A tangled vine with thick stalks and floppy leaves covered the ground and climbed the trees.

"It looks like a jungle in the movies," Terry said.

Max found a loose board in the fence. "We could pry this off and slip through to explore the jungle."

Terry thought this was a great idea, but they never had a chance to try it.

And now Mr. Robertson was starting to hit the rotten wood at the bottom of the fence with a big hammer. Some of the old boards broke and fell into the yard.

"Look, Dad. A mountain of dirt is piled up behind the fence!" Max said.

"Not just dirt. Here's something that looks like part of an older fence. And what's this?" His father dragged out a set of broken slats nailed together.

"Maybe it was a trellis," Mrs. Robertson said.

"What's a trellis, Mom?" Terry asked.

"That's a frame for roses to climb on," her mother told her.

"Dad," Max said, "how many different fences do you think have been built here?"

Mr. Robertson picked up a shovel and dug out a pile of dirt, a rusty pipe, and part of a red brick. "Probably a great many, Max. No fence could last long with all this junk pushing against it. I'm going to build a wall."

"That will take much more work than putting up a fence, George," Mrs. Robertson reminded her husband.

"There's a new type of wall built of

stones made to fit together," Mr. Robertson said. "You don't have to use cement, and it's the best type of wall to hold back dirt. I'm going to go over to that building supply place on Fifteenth Avenue and order the stone. Do you want to come and choose the color?"

"Oh, Dad," Max begged. "May I come, too?"

"No, Max," his father answered. "You and Terry would be begging me to buy everything in the store. Your mom and I will do better alone. Come along, Betty." He put down the shovel and walked to the back door of the house.

"We won't be long," Mrs. Robertson told the children. She rushed after her husband.

2

Terry picked up a broken slat and scraped at the dirt coming through the break Mr. Robertson had made in the fence. "Dad's going to build a stone wall. Now we'll never be able to go exploring."

Max nodded. "I know."

Terry jammed the slat into the dirt and twisted it. "We should have gone through the fence yesterday when you found one of the boards was loose."

"Don't be silly, Terry," her brother said. "We're lucky we didn't pry the board off the fence. We'd have all this junk blocking our way on the other side. We couldn't get through the fence and we'd have a job nailing the board back."

Terry picked up the shovel. She began to dig at the dirt through the broken fence. "Maybe we can make a tunnel. This stuff doesn't seem too hard."

Max pointed at the dirt. "Put down the shovel, Terry," he whispered.

Terry couldn't believe her eyes. The dirt she had been digging was moving all by itself. It twirled round and round and started to become a kind of funnel going sideways through the fence.

As it whirled, the hole in the middle of the dirt became larger. The whirling whistled like a wind now.

Then, suddenly, the whirling stopped and all was quiet. There was a little tunnel going through the ground behind the fence.

Terry looked at her brother.

"Are you scared?" he asked.

"No, but I don't know why I'm not scared," Terry told him. "This is magic, isn't it?"

Max nodded. "It's funny. I thought I'd stopped believing in magic, but I sure believe in it now."

"Then, what are we waiting for?" Terry got down on her hands and knees and started to crawl through the tunnel.

Max followed his sister. "I guess you're right, Terry. After all, this may be our last chance to see what's on the other side of the fence."

The tunnel was just big enough for the children to crawl through. It was damp and cool under the ground. They could see a faint light somewhere in front of them. It seemed close, but they had to crawl for quite a while before they reached the end of the tunnel.

Terry scrambled out onto soft damp weeds. She stood up and stretched. Then she bent over to grab her brother's hand and pull him out of the tunnel.

Max turned to look back at it. "Terry, it's gone!"

The ground was as green and weedy as if there had never been a tunnel there.

3

"I'm not sure how we're going to get back into our yard again," Max said.

Terry looked around. "The tunnel seems to have taken us into the middle of the jungle. There are so many trees here that I can't see any of the houses."

"Well, we wanted to explore. We'd better get started." Max walked toward a clump of tall flat grass and fuzzy brown cattails.

Terry followed him. The ground under her feet felt soft and spongy. She saw Max reach the cattails, then try to step back. He lost his balance, slid into the tall grass, and disappeared.

"Watch out, Terry," he yelled. "There's water here!"

Terry had to push the cattails aside to see her brother.

Max had slid down a slippery bank and was standing ankle-deep in a clear running stream.

"It's perfect for wading," he said, "but I'd better get my sneakers off."

Terry lay flat on the ground. She held onto the cattail stems with one hand and took hold of Max's hand with the other.

He climbed back up the bank and sat down to take off his sneakers. Terry hurried to take hers off, too. It was August, and they were both wearing shorts.

Terry left her sneakers beside the cattails. "I won't have to bother with them while I'm wading."

Max put his wet sneakers on a flat rock. Then they both stepped into the shallow stream. Water striders played on the surface. The water was deeper in the middle of the stream. They heard a splash.

Terry pointed. "Look, Max!"

A fish leaped up after a water strider.

"Too bad I didn't bring my drop-line," Max said.

The stream wound along. Enormous trees lined the mossy banks. A kingfisher swooped down from an overhanging branch and snatched fish from the water.

They were wading downstream. The water was higher than Terry's knees now. Something brushed against her legs. "Max, I'm caught on something! I can't walk."

Max waded over to her. "It's some kind of net. We'd better go back." He pulled the web of cords away from Terry's legs.

They started wading back upstream. Terry kept looking for the clump of cattails where she had left her shoes. There were more cattails than she remembered, but none of them were next to her sneakers.

At last, Max said, "There are the skid marks I made in the bank. This is the place, Terry."

"It's the place all right," Terry whispered. "But look over by that tree. Someone has picked up my shoes!"

4

Someone was standing in the shadow of an enormous pine tree holding Terry's bright red sneakers and staring at them.

Max took his sneakers off the rock and began to put them on.

Terry ran barefoot over to the tree. As she came closer to it, she saw that the person with her sneakers was a very young woman. She was saying, "Pretty! Pretty!" and was so busy admiring the sneakers that she didn't notice Terry.

"I think they're pretty, too," Terry said. "But my mom doesn't like them."

When the woman caught sight of Terry, her mouth fell open, and her dark eyes opened wide. She even seemed afraid to move.

"Please, may I have my sneakers?" Terry took them from the woman and bent down to put them on her feet.

"Oh, they're moccasins!" the woman said. She wasn't afraid now.

When Max walked over to join them, the woman looked from one to the other. "You are both washed-out looking!" she said. "I was afraid you were spirits. Now I see that you are Lenape but not Leni-Lenape. Is it some kind of sickness that makes the color fade from your hair and skin?"

Neither Max nor Terry knew what to say. Max had blue eyes and blond hair. Terry's eyes were green. Her hair was light brown and wavy. They looked at the woman. Her skin was a dark rosy

tan, and her hair, worn in two braids, was straight and black and shiny. She was neither fat nor thin. She wore a sleeveless blouse and a knee-length wraparound skirt with fringes at the bottom. Both her clothes and her shoes were made of soft leather.

"My name is Singing-Moon," she said. "What's yours?"

"I'm Max," he said. "And this is my sister, Terry."

A board dangled from one of the short bare branches on the lower part of the pine tree. Terry walked over to it. "Who is this?"

Max came over to look.

A baby in a leather pouch that laced up the front was strapped to the board.

A little roof over his head protected him from sun and wind. Tiny spinning objects dangled from the roof to keep the baby amused.

"That's my little darling," Singing-Moon told them.

"What's his name?" Max asked.

"He's not old enough yet to tell us what it is," Singing-Moon said.

"Do all children in your family get a chance to choose their own names?" Max wanted to know.

Singing-Moon laughed. "Of course!"

"How do they pick them?" Terry asked.

"Something happens to them or they have a dream. Later on they can change their names. It is strange that you don't know our ways," Singing-Moon said. "You must have come from far away. Sit down and tell me about it."

5

Singing-Moon sat on the mossy ground under the big pine tree.

Terry and Max sat facing her.

Max spoke first. "We wanted to see what was on the other side of the fence behind our house. There was so much dirt behind the fence that Terry decided to dig a tunnel through it."

"What's a tunnel?" Singing-Moon asked.

"A kind of long cave with an opening at each end," Terry told her. "I started to dig and then the dirt swirled around and dug a magic tunnel all by itself. I crawled through and Max came after me."

"But when I turned to look back at the tunnel, it was gone," Max said.

Singing-Moon nodded. "Magic is like that. You never know what it will do. I will talk to my grandfather about it. He is the chief of our village and is very wise. Perhaps you should change your names. Would you like to be Cave-Crawler and Traveler-Through-Tunnels?"

"Maybe later, if that's the only thing that will work," Max said. "For now I'll keep my old name."

A wind was shaking the branches of the pine tree. A long thin pinecone tumbled into Terry's lap. Singing-Moon picked it up and looked at it. "Just ripe." She pulled a basket of braided grass from under a bush and began to search the ground under the tree for more pinecones.

Whenever a gust of wind came along, more cones rained down from above.

Terry and Max joined Singing-Moon in gathering them.

When they had scooped up all the cones they could see, Singing-Moon took her baby off the tree and tied him to her back with a woven strap. The strap went around her forehead and left Singing-Moon's arms free.

She started to pick up the basket of pinecones, but Terry stopped her. "I'll carry that for you."

Singing-Moon smiled. "Very good. I was hoping you would come home with me. Max should have some sort of spear or club in case we meet a bobcat or a bear."

"I have something better." Max pulled a slingshot from the back pocket of his shorts. He had made the slingshot himself and used it with spitballs for target practice in the basement at home.

He went to the stream for smooth round stones. Max was certain spitballs would not be the best things to use for shooting bears and bobcats.

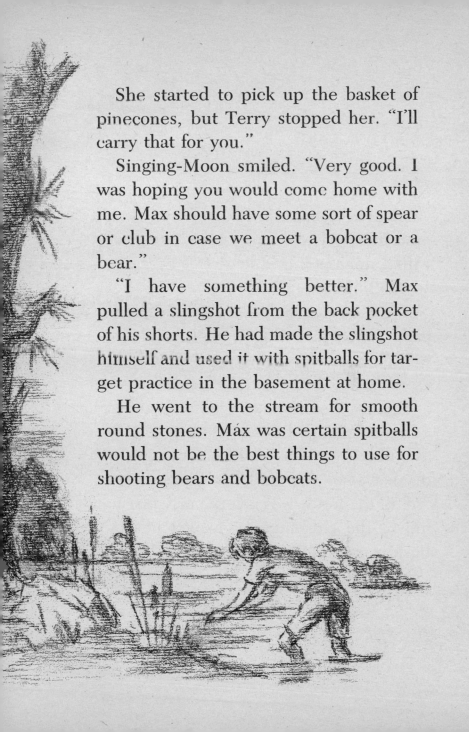

6

Singing-Moon reached behind the pine tree and took out a wooden spear with a stone point. "I keep this near me all the time."

She led Max and Terry to a narrow path. It was just wide enough for them to walk one behind the other. The trees grew close together on each side.

Singing-Moon walked without making a sound. Max and Terry tried to be just as quiet. They were careful not to rustle dry leaves or step on fallen twigs.

Still the forest was a very noisy place, full of the chirpings of many kinds of birds and insects.

When they came to a little open space

between the trees, they heard a rustling
in the underbrush.

Singing-Moon stopped before she
went into the clearing. She pointed her
spear in the direction of the rustling
sound.

Max fitted a stone into his slingshot.

Terry held tight to the basket and felt
her heart thumping in her chest.

The rustling became louder. Suddenly
a doe with a spotted fawn burst out of
the bushes. They leaped across the little

glade, bobbing their white tails, and disappeared into the forest.

Singing-Moon rested the wooden end of the spear on the ground for a few minutes before going on.

She must have been just as scared as I was, Terry said to herself.

The baby was fast asleep and missed all the excitement.

The path through the forest went in the same direction as the stream. After a while the trees became farther apart.

Max and Terry saw clearings where corn was growing. The cornstalks were planted three or four feet apart. Beans of many colors were growing up the cornstalks and using them for beanpoles. In between the rows of corn were squash, pumpkins, and watermelons.

Soon there were planting fields all along the stream.

Singing-Moon led them to a tall stockade fence. The gate was open.

"This is my village," Singing-Moon said. "Come inside."

In the center of the village was an open space. A mound in it was higher than the rest of the ground.

There were about ten houses within the fence. Each house had been made from a circle of young trees tied together in a dome shape. The houses were covered with strips of birch bark, animal skins, or mats woven of cattail reeds. Some were covered with all three. They had no windows, but each house had four doors and a hole in the roof to let the smoke out.

Singing-Moon led Terry and Max to the largest house. "I want you to meet Wise-Defender, our chief."

7

The mats used to cover the four doorways were folded back. A gentle breeze blew through the house.

Singing-Moon stepped inside. Terry and Max followed her into the shadowy room.

A small smoky fire was burning in a circle of smoke-stained stones.

Strings of corn held together by braided husks were tied to a pole that went across the ceiling. Bunches of dried herbs, clumps of roots, and strips of dried pumpkin also hung from the pole. They were all drying in the smoke from the fire.

Terry and Max heard the sound of gentle snoring. They looked around and saw a thin old man fast asleep on one of the low benches that went around the walls.

Singing-Moon went over to him. She bent down and pressed her cheek against his hand.

The old man opened his eyes. When he saw Singing-Moon, he sat up and hugged her. The children saw that his white hair reached to his shoulders.

"I'm sorry I had to wake you, Grandfather," Singing-Moon said.

"I'm glad you did. I was having a bad dream. I dreamed that the forest was gone from here, and so was the stream. Our people were gone, too." He laughed. "I'm glad it was only a dream."

"So am I, Grandfather," Singing-Moon said. "I woke you because I want you to meet my friends and hear their

31

strange story. This is Max, and this is Terry." She turned to the children. "And this is our chief, Wise-Defender."

The old man stood up and smiled. He held out both hands to each of them, and they gave him theirs in return.

He had such a kind face that Terry and Max liked him at once.

"I must go and feed my little darling," Singing-Moon said to the children. "I'll come back for you afterward." She left the house with the baby on her back and her spear still in her hand.

Wise-Defender sat down on the bench again. The ground in front of him was covered with soft pine branches. Terry

and Max decided to sit there, so they could look at him while they talked.

"Start at the very beginning," Wise-Defender said. "The more I learn about you, the better chance I'll have of understanding what happened."

Together they told him as much as they remembered. "We only wanted to know what was behind our fence," Max finished.

"I think you're beginning to find out," Wise-Defender told him.

8

When Singing-Moon returned, Wise-Defender lay down again on the bench and closed his eyes.

Terry and Max followed Singing-Moon out of the house to a much smaller one.

"Does your grandfather live all by himself?" Terry asked.

"Oh, no," Singing-Moon told her. "Two of my aunts and their families live with him. Wise-Defender is very old and needs people to care for him. My husband and I built a house of our own. You must stay with us."

A young man was standing in front of the little house, holding the baby in the air and dancing with him.

"This is my husband, Blackbird-on-the-Wing," Singing-Moon said. "And these are our guests, Terry and Max," she told him.

"Welcome," the young man said. "Look at this!" He leaned over and let the baby's tiny feet touch the ground. At once the baby straightened his legs and tried to stand. His father laughed and lifted his son into the air again. "Not yet, little man," he said, "but you'll get there!"

Blackbird-on-the-Wing had heard about the slingshot and wanted to see it. Max took it out of his pocket and showed him how the slingshot worked.

A fire burned in front of each house. People were cooking and eating there.

Singing-Moon was busy at her fire. Terry went to help her.

She saw a pile of clean smooth stones near the fire.

Singing-Moon kept taking stones from the pile and putting them into the fire. Terry copied her. She learned to use two sticks to pull the hot stones out of the fire and drop them into a large wooden bowl of water.

When the water in the wooden bowl began to boil, Singing-Moon used a stone knife to skin and cut up two rabbits Blackbird-on-the-Wing had caught in his snares, and a large fish he'd speared, along with all sorts of roots and leafy wild plants. She dropped everything into the bowl and added several handfuls of cornmeal. Terry kept the water bubbling by putting in more hot stones.

"Do you always use wooden bowls?" Terry asked.

Singing-Moon showed her clay pots that were black from many fires. These had pointed bottoms, which had to be propped up by hot stones when they were in the fire.

The pinecones they had gathered were now on a slab of birch bark. They had started to open and drop their seeds onto the bark. Singing-Moon scooped up as many seeds as she could and dropped them into the bowl of boiling water. She stirred the mixture with a long wooden paddle.

9

The baby was asleep in his leather pouch on the board swinging from the maple tree next to the little house.

When the food in the wooden bowl was cooked, Blackbird-on-the-Wing sat on the ground beside it. "Are you hungry?"

The children nodded.

"Sit." Singing-Moon handed each of them a large clamshell, gave one to her husband, and kept one for herself.

They sat near the big bowl and used the clamshells to scoop out the food. Terry and Max had never tasted anything quite like it. They enjoyed some of the things in the mixture more than others. Nobody told them what to eat or made them finish anything they didn't like.

Terry and Max ate what they wanted and stopped when they'd had enough.

All the people in the village seemed to be out-of-doors in front of their houses. Some of them were eating. Some were making mats, stretching leather, carving wood, or doing other kinds of work.

Children were playing games. A girl not quite as tall as Max came over with a younger boy to meet Max and Terry. "We want you to be happy here," the girl said. "Tomorrow we can show you a good place to go swimming."

It was getting dark. The people went into their houses.

Terry looked up at a sky that was filled with more stars than she had ever seen in Brooklyn. "Look, Max!"

Max stared up at them. "Terry," he

whispered, "the stars are in exactly the same place in the sky that they are at home. It's just that, without all the lights, we can see them better."

"What does that mean?" Terry asked.

"It means we're still in the same place, but I've a feeling we're in a different time."

"I've read about that in stories, but I never really believed it," Terry said.

"It's all part of the magic," Max reminded her. "Singing-Moon seemed to think all we had to do was change our names to go home again. But I like it here, and I'm not ready to be called Traveler-Through-Tunnels."

"Won't Mom and Dad be looking for us?" Terry said.

Max thought about this. "We can't do anything about it, Terry. We'll just have to see what happens."

Singing-Moon had taken her baby into

the house. Now she came out to tell the children, "It's not safe to be out at night. Come inside, and I'll show you where you can sleep."

In the house a small fire glowed under drying herbs and corn.

Singing-Moon showed them where soft animal skins had been spread over the benches that went around the walls.

"Ow!" Max slapped his bare arm.

Singing-Moon gave him a clay pot of some sort of ointment. "This will keep mosquitoes away."

Both Max and Terry rubbed the ointment on themselves. Then they curled up on the soft skins and fell asleep.

10

Singing-Moon woke the children in the morning. "Get up," she said. "Snow-Flower and Like-a-Possum have come to take you to their swimming place."

Terry sat up and looked around. For a minute she didn't know where she was.

"Like-a-what?" Max asked.

"Like-a-Possum." Singing-Moon laughed. "That's the name he chose. You're not the only one who thinks it's funny. He and Snow-Flower are my cousin's children."

Terry stood up and stretched.

"The water in our stream is good to drink," Singing-Moon told her. "There's a flat rock next to the stream near the little willow trees."

Terry went outside. "I'll be ready soon," she said to the two children who were waiting at the door.

Terry ran over to the stream. She kneeled on the flat rock, leaned over the water, and cupped her hands to get a drink. Then she splashed water on her face and combed her hair with her wet fingers.

Max came over to meet his sister. "If you want breakfast, you'd better eat something now," he told her. "I was talking to Blackbird-on-the-Wing. These people don't have regular mealtimes. They just eat when they're hungry." Max showed Terry a little bag of woven hemp. "He gave me this and said there's something in it we can chew when we're hungry and can't find any nuts or berries. He takes a bag of this stuff when he goes hunting. He says he can't do without it."

Terry decided she'd better eat while she had a chance. She went back to the little house. Singing-Moon was sitting under the maple tree feeding her baby.

Snow-Flower had a fire burning and was heating stones in it. Terry joined her. Together they re-warmed the food in the wooden bowl. By the time it was ready, the baby was asleep in his little pouch on the board, swinging from the maple tree.

Blackbird-on-the-Wing and the two boys sat down by the bowl, along with Terry and Snow-Flower. Singing-Moon brought out six clamshells, and everybody scooped out what they wanted.

A little dog with pointed ears came over and sat down to watch them eat.

Terry and Max saw that Blackbird-on-the-Wing tossed the food he didn't want to the dog. So did Like-a-Possum and Snow-Flower. Max started to copy them, and then Terry did the same.

"Singing-Moon eats everything," Terry whispered to her brother.

"Just like Mom," he said.

11

When the meal was over, Singing-Moon showed Max and Terry how to wipe the clamshells clean with dried grass. Then she gave each of them a sack of strong hemp. "Carry this everywhere. You can put what you gather into it."

Terry saw that both Snow-Flower and Like-a-Possum carried sacks. Snow-Flower also had a thick stick. Like-a-Possum held a short spear. They led the way through the village. Snow-Flower introduced Terry and Max to the people they met. Everybody seemed to be her aunt or uncle or cousin. They all stopped what they were doing to greet the visitors.

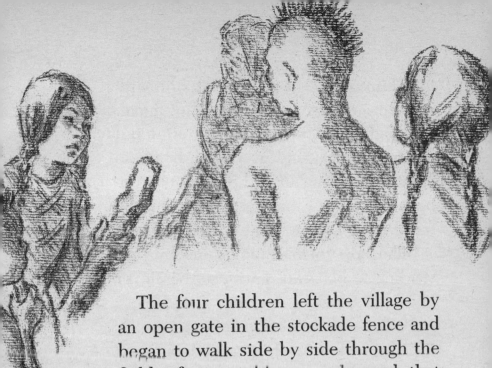

The four children left the village by
an open gate in the stockade fence and
began to walk side by side through the
fields of corn and beans and squash that
were planted along the stream.

"Why did you pick Like-a-Possum for
your name?" Max wanted to know.

"One day I saw a possum sleeping in
a tree," the younger boy told him. "I left
my spear under the tree and quietly
climbed up to grab him.

"I put the possum in my sack and carried him down to the ground. When I

took him out of the sack to kill him with my spear, he was stiff and didn't move. I thought he'd been smothered. I put down the spear and used both hands to open the sack again and put the possum back into it. But that possum was up the tree before I knew what was happening.

"The possum had fooled me by pretending to be dead. I want to be clever like him. So I changed my name."

"What was it before?" Max asked.

"Little-Cloud," Like-a-Possum told him.

Max thought about this. "You were right to change it."

They crossed the last planting field and began to follow the narrow path that led downstream.

The path led through the woods. Snow-Flower went first. Max came after her. Like-a-Possum followed him, and Terry was last.

They walked silently. When they came to a large oak tree, Like-a-Possum pointed to piles of acorns lying on the ground under it. "We'd better gather these to take home."

"Why do you want them?" Terry asked.

"To make bread," he told her.

Max looked at the acorns. "If we get them on our way home, we won't have to carry them all day."

"They might not be here later," Snow-Flower said.

Suddenly Max saw something orange and brown and shiny among the acorns. It was long and thin and it was moving toward him. When it raised its head he saw that it was a copperhead snake.

He'd learned in Boy Scouts that copperheads are deadly!

12

Pow! A stone went flying from the slingshot in Max's hand. It struck the copperhead right in the teeth.

Snow-Flower banged the snake on the head with her club.

When the snake stopped moving, Like-a-Possum said, "He's dead now, Max. Put him in your sack. You can make a belt or a headband from his skin."

"You can have it," Max told him.

Like-a-Possum dropped the dead snake into his sack.

Terry walked over to her brother. "I don't know how you did it, Max. I was too scared to move."

Max looked at the slingshot. "I'm still scared, Terry. I'd forgotten all about the slingshot and was thinking about acorns. I don't remember putting the stone in the slingshot."

Terry bent down and started to pick up acorns and drop them into her sack. Max joined her, but he kept his slingshot handy.

When they'd collected all the acorns they could find, the four children continued along the narrow path. But now everybody kept looking for snakes.

The trees became farther apart. Soon the path was crossing a wide plain with only a single big tree in sight.

Snow-Flower ran over to a clump of scrubby bushes. She popped something into her mouth. "Yum!"

The others joined her in eating the ripe blueberries. These were much smaller than the ones Mrs. Robertson bought in the stores, but they tasted wonderful.

They ate all the blueberries they could find. Then Terry found a patch of blackberries. They were bigger and juicier than the blueberries, but the children had to watch out for thorns.

After everyone had eaten enough berries, they went back to the path leading across the plain.

The sun was high in the sky now. It was warmer here than in the forest. Snow-Flower began to walk faster. She led the way to a large pond surrounded by reeds and cattails. "Here we are! This is the best place to swim."

Terry and Max heard the sound of splashing and laughing voices. When they came to the shore of the pond, they saw groups of children playing in the clear water.

Snow-Flower and Like-a-Possum took off their moccasins. Terry and Max slipped out of their sneakers. They left them with the rest of their things on a bank overlooking the water.

"Last one in is a rotten pumpkin!" Like-a-Possum dashed toward the pond.

The others chased after him.

13

The pond was deep enough for them to swim, but not so deep that it was dangerous. Most of the children were good swimmers, but some were teaching themselves how to swim.

The smaller ones bobbed like corks in the water. The older ones swam like ducks, diving down and kicking their feet in the air.

Like-a-Possum wanted to race with Max, but Max won. He had longer arms and legs to push back the water.

Snow-Flower was good at swimming underwater.

"Show me how you do that," Terry said. "I always seem to be up on top. You swim like a fish."

Snow-Flower showed her how she swam. No matter how hard she tried to copy her, Terry still floated to the surface.

Snow-Flower watched her, "Terry, you don't need to swim! I see you sitting in the water, turning around on your back or your stomach, and not sinking no matter what you do. If I stop swimming, I sink. I wish I could float like you."

They raced each other across the pond. Snow-Flower kept swimming, but Terry would roll over to look at the sky and drift. Snow-Flower had reached the other side of the pond and was on the way back before Terry was near it.

While they were swimming, a few clouds began to gather. The sky became darker. A drop of rain fell on Terry's nose.

"We'd better start for home!" Max yelled. He swam to shore.

The others were quick to follow him. As soon as they were ready, all four picked up their sacks. Like-a-Possum grabbed his spear. Snow-Flower held onto her club, and Max made sure his slingshot was ready. Terry was glad she didn't have a weapon. She didn't want to have to kill anything.

They left the pond and started back across the open plain. The rain was coming down harder, and the sky was almost black.

Terry saw a flash of lightning in a cloud. A moment later they all heard the rumble of thunder.

They passed the blackberry patches and the blueberry bushes. The rain was coming down in torrents now.

Up ahead towered a lonely tree.

"Just what we need!" Like-a-Possum ran over to take shelter under the spreading branches.

Terry threw down her sack. She raced over to drag him back into the pouring rain.

"What's the matter with you?" Like-a-Possum struggled to get away from her.

Suddenly there was a blinding light and a deafening boom. A fork of lightning had split the trunk of the tree in half!

Nobody said anything for a while. Then Terry picked up her sack. "Didn't anybody ever warn you guys not to stand under a tree in the rain?"

14

Snow-Flower led the way through the pouring rain. Max noticed that there were places where the narrow path became two paths. It would be easy to lose their way. He was glad they had Snow-Flower for a guide.

The thunder rumbled away into the distant clouds. The sky became lighter. Before they reached the forest, the rain stopped, and the sun came out.

"I'm glad," Like-a-Possum said. "I wasn't going to walk under all those trees while it was still raining."

Water dripped from the trees at first. Farther along, the woods were dry. When they came to the oak tree, they saw more acorns. A gray squirrel was

busy burying some of them.

Like-a-Possum grabbed Max's arm and silently pointed first to the slingshot and then to the squirrel

Max shook his head.

The squirrel saw him, flicked his tail, and scampered up the tree.

Like-a-Possum was disappointed. "You could have shot him easily, Max. Why didn't you?"

Max used to feed peanuts to squirrels. He couldn't hurt one.

"The slingshot is magic," Terry said. "It only does what it wants to."

Nobody argued about this. And nobody wanted to pick up more acorns. They left them for the squirrel and walked quickly along the path.

Terry began to feel empty inside. "Those berries were good," she said, "but they didn't fill me up."

Max took out the little bag Blackbird-on-the-Wing had given him. "I'm hungry, too. How about you guys?"

Snow-Flower and Like-a-Possum each took a handful of dry cornmeal out of the bag and began to chew it.

Terry grabbed a handful and popped it into her mouth. It was so dry she thought she would choke, but she kept chewing until the cornmeal became moist. Then it began to taste good. Soon it was soft enough to eat. Terry's stomach felt much better. She looked at Max. He was still chewing. And he looked surprised.

It was a long walk through the woods. The sky was turning pink by the time they reached the stockade fence around the village.

Singing-Moon and her grandfather were waiting at the gate. Her baby was on Singing-Moon's back.

"Run home!" Wise-Defender told Snow-Flower and Like-a-Possum. "Your mother is waiting for you."

They raced off to their own house.

Singing-Moon was surprised that the children were so wet. It had not rained here.

Wise-Defender led the way to Singing-Moon's house. He went to sit near her cooking fire. "Come over here and dry those damp clothes," he told Terry and Max.

15

Singing-Moon took the acorns Max and Terry had in their sacks. She put them into a clay pot that had a pointed bottom. Then she filled the pot with water and ashes. She dropped stones into the fire and used them to prop up the pot.

She brought out a fur robe for each of the children to wear while their shorts and T-shirts were drying by the fire.

Her grandfather was sitting next to Terry and Max. "Now tell us what happened to you today."

First Terry told Singing-Moon and Wise-Defender about the copperhead snake hiding in the acorns and how Max killed the snake with his slingshot.

"You should change your name to Quick-and-Brave," Singing-Moon said.

Max shook his head. "I was scared stiff. Terry thinks the slingshot is magic."

"Let me see it." Wise-Defender reached for the slingshot.

Max fitted a stone into the wide rubber band and handed him the slingshot.

Wise-Defender took aim at the lowest branch of the maple tree and let fly.

Pow! The stone crashed into the branch.

"Thief! Thief!" A startled bluejay flew out of the tree.

Wise-Defender handed back the slingshot. "I don't know if it's magic, but it's better than a bow and arrow for killing snakes."

Max told how Terry had dragged Like-a-Possum away from the tree in the thunderstorm.

"Terry!" Singing-Moon stared at her. "How did you know the lightning would split the tree? Is this more magic?"

"I didn't know," Terry said. "I was taught that lightning strikes the tallest things around. That was the only tree there."

When Singing-Moon learned that they'd eaten nothing but berries and cornmeal, she heated stones and warmed a stew.

Wise-Defender stayed to eat with them. Blackbird-on-the-Wing came home in time to join them. He had spent the day building a deadfall trap for a bear. Max wanted to know what a dead-fall was, but Blackbird-on-the-Wing laughed. "It's different each time. I have to trick the bear into making very heavy logs fall on him. Would you like to come with me tomorrow when I go hunting? I can show you the trap then."

Max was excited. "I'd like very much to go," he said.

Terry was happy that she had not been invited.

16

Early next morning, Max left to go hunting with Blackbird-on-the-Wing.

Terry looked into the wooden bowl where the acorns had been soaking in water and wood ashes. She saw that the shells had fallen off the kernels. They were like little nuts now.

She helped Singing-Moon rinse the kernels in clear water and spread them on a flat stone to dry in the sun.

Later in the day Singing-Moon and Terry took turns using a stone pounder in the hollow of a small log to grind the kernels into acorn flour. Singing-Moon mixed the flour with water to make little flat loaves of acorn bread. She wrapped the loaves in vine leaves and baked them in the hot ashes of her cooking fire.

Some of the corn in the planting field was ripe. Terry went with Singing-Moon to help pick it. They hung the baby in his pouch from the lowest branch of a persimmon tree next to the field. He laughed when he swung back and forth as the breeze swayed the branch.

Singing-Moon showed Terry which ears of corn were ripe. She put them into the sack she'd used for the acorns the day before.

When they were ready to take the

corn to the house, the baby was fast asleep. Singing-Moon put him on her back again.

They picked a few of the biggest ears to roast in their husks.

Singing-Moon showed Terry how to braid together the husks of the corn to be dried. They strung these from the pole above the little fire in the house.

After Singing-Moon fed her baby, she hung his pouch on the maple tree and brought out some patties made of cornmeal and maple syrup.

Terry was so hungry that the sticky patty tasted wonderful.

Singing-Moon nibbled hers happily. "I never want to eat anything after this." When she'd eaten the last crumb, she licked her fingers. "You must be thirsty. I know I am. Let's get a drink." Singing-Moon ran over to the flat rock by the stream.

Terry followed her. They kneeled down and cupped their hands to drink the cool clear water.

"I should have brought the water carrier," Singing-Moon said. "We will need fresh water for cooking."

"I'll get it," Terry told her.

The water container was stored under one of the benches inside the house. It was carved of wood and was heavy. There was a leather carrying strap. Terry slipped it over her shoulder. She had to make several trips to the stream before she had enough water to fill Singing-Moon's clay pots and her big wooden bowl.

Singing-Moon started heating stones in the fire in front of her house. The water in the bowl was boiling by the time Max and Blackbird-on-the-Wing returned from the hunt.

17

Max was excited. "Look what we caught!"

Terry saw that he was carrying a string of fish. "I thought you were going bear hunting."

"The bear was smarter than I was," Blackbird-on-the-Wing told her. "He must have knocked over the heavy logs with his paw. Then he ate the bait and went away."

"I'm glad he didn't wait for you," Singing-Moon said.

"So am I!" Her husband hugged her.

"When we went upstream, we saw fish jumping right out of the water,"

Max said. "Blackbird-on-the-Wing tried shooting them with his bow and arrow, but the fish were too quick. I dug some worms, and Blackbird-on-the-Wing had a couple of bone fishhooks and some twine in that leather bag tied to his belt."

"It would have been more fun to get the fish with my bow and arrow," Blackbird-on-the-Wing told them.

Singing-Moon cleaned and cut up the fish. She dropped them into the water in the wooden bowl. Terry added more hot rocks to keep the water boiling.

Terry saw Singing-Moon lift one of the slabs of bark on the ground near the house. Under it was a round hole lined with mats of woven reeds. Singing-Moon took out roots, cornmeal, dried herbs, and berries, and put them into the bowl with the fish. Terry helped by putting the slab back on the hole.

Max and Terry enjoyed the stew more

than the one they'd had the night before. Max thought it was because he was getting used to this sort of food. Terry knew it was because she'd helped prepare it.

Before they finished eating, Terry heard a *boom-boom-boom*. "What's that?"

"Our drum," Blackbird-on-the-Wing said. "Do you like to dance?"

"I do, but Max doesn't," Terry told him.

Like-a-Possum came running over to where they were sitting near the fire. His eyes were shining. "Come on. They're getting ready to start!"

Boom, boom, boom! The booming continued.

"I keep chewing to the beat of that drum," Max told Terry.

It was a haunting sound. Terry felt as if it were calling her. She stood up and helped Singing-Moon wipe the clamshells and put them away.

"Hurry!" Like-a-Possum begged. "They're already starting."

"That shouldn't bother you," Blackbird-on-the-Wing told him. "You may join the dance whenever you want to."

"It's just that I hate to miss any of it," Like-a-Possum said. "It's been ages since we had a dance."

Blackbird-on-the-Wing laughed. "Run along then and start dancing. We'll see you later."

18

Singing-Moon strapped her baby on her back. She walked with Blackbird-on-the-Wing toward the open space in the middle of the village. Terry and Max came after them. On the way they met Wise-Defender and Snow-Flower going to the dance.

"The sound of the drum makes me want to dance," Snow-Flower said.

"It makes me feel young again," her great-grandfather told them.

A bonfire was blazing in the clearing where the dance was going on. Everybody in the village seemed to be there. Like-a-Possum was already dancing.

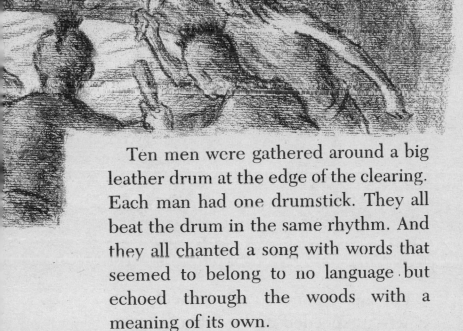

Ten men were gathered around a big leather drum at the edge of the clearing. Each man had one drumstick. They all beat the drum in the same rhythm. And they all chanted a song with words that seemed to belong to no language but echoed through the woods with a meaning of its own.

The dancers began or stopped dancing as they chose. The line of dancers moved clockwise around the clearing. Each dancer made up his own dance steps, but all the steps beat in rhythm with the drum. Max and Terry didn't have any trouble keeping up.

For some dances the drum beat more slowly. It speeded up for others. Snow-Flower wiggled and squirmed all the way through the snake dance. When the turkey dance was played, almost everybody flapped their arms.

During some dances the drum was silent. The singers chanted in a rhythm for the dancers to follow.

Singing-Moon's baby bounced up and down and chirped with joy. At last he fell asleep.

Blackbird-on-the-Wing stepped out of the line of dancers and signed to his wife that the baby was asleep. Singing-Moon moved away from the dance. Max and Terry followed her.

"You can go on dancing if you want to," Singing-Moon told them. "We're going to bed."

Terry looked at Max. "What about it?"

"I never thought I'd like dancing, but this is fun," he said. "I'd like to dance a while longer."

Terry grinned. "Me, too."

"We'll see you in the morning — if you're awake." Blackbird-on-the-Wing and Singing-Moon took their baby home.

Max and Terry stepped back into the moving line of dancers. For another hour they followed the rhythm of the drum and of the strange chant.

Even after they were asleep in the little house, Terry still heard the haunting music in her dreams.

19

Next morning, Like-a-Possum came over to tell everybody the news of the day. "They're heating stones for the sweat lodge! I'm going to take a steam bath."

"I'd better take one," Blackbird-on-the-Wing said. He turned to Max and Terry. "What about you two? Steam baths are good for your health."

"What's a sweat lodge?" Terry asked.

Singing-Moon was busy with her baby. "Go with Blackbird-on-the-Wing," she said. "He will show you."

Like-a-Possum dashed on ahead.

Terry and Max followed Blackbird-on-the-Wing around the inside of the stockade fence. When they came to an open gate, they saw that the stream was close to the other side of the fence.

On the ground near the gate was a small dome made like the roofs of the houses. Blackbird-on-the-Wing lifted it off the ground. Under the dome they saw a big hole lined with clay and stones. "This is the sweat lodge."

Two men were heating bundles of stones in a fire close to the lodge. A woman kept coming through the gate from the stream with armloads of wet leaves.

When the stones were hot, the men

dropped them into the hole and covered them with the leaves. They closed the hole with the dome and waited until clouds of steam seeped out.

The men used long sticks to take out the stones.

Blackbird-on-the-Wing held the dome while the woman and the two men climbed into the hole. He watched Like-a-Possum scramble down. Then he slipped inside and lowered the dome over his head.

Terry was frightened. "Max! He'll be smothered!"

Max was worried, too, but he didn't want Terry to know it. "Blackbird-on-the-Wing knows what he's doing. He'll be okay."

They stood and watched the steam drifting out of the cracks in the dome. It seemed forever before someone shoved the dome off the hole.

One of the two men who had heated the stones climbed out. He was dripping with sweat, but he turned around to lift Like-a-Possum out of the hole.

The woman who collected the wet leaves was next. Then came the other heater of stones. At last Blackbird-on-the-Wing burst into view. He was so covered with sweat that he gleamed in the bright sunlight.

Without a word, he leaped out of the hole, dashed to the gate, and jumped into the cool stream.

First Like-a-Possum, and then the woman and the two men who had shared the sweat lodge with him, followed Blackbird-on-the-Wing into the water.

Max stared at them. "It must be good for their health. They all look better than they did before."

Terry laughed. "That's because they're clean now."

20

Most of the people in the village took turns using the sweat lodge. They kept heating stones and covering them with wet leaves.

"Maybe we should try it," Max said.

"Some other day," Terry told him. "Let's go see if Singing-Moon thinks it's time to eat."

Singing-Moon was boiling ears of corn in their husks. She pulled them out of the water with flat sticks. Terry and Max had to let the husks cool before they could strip them off the ears. Blackbird-on-the-Wing came home in time to join in eating them.

The beans and squash and pumpkins as well as the corn were ripening in the planting fields. For days Terry worked with all the women and girls in the village to gather and store the food. Much of it was hung to dry in the smoke over the fires in the houses.

Every day Max went with Blackbird-on-the-Wing to hunt rabbits, squirrels, beavers, partridges, ducks, and geese. One day he watched a heavy wild turkey fly across an open field. When it fell down, tired from flying, Max caught the turkey in his hands.

Another day he went along on a deer hunt with all the men and boys from the village. The boys each had a flat bone and a stick to beat it with. They stood a hundred paces apart in the forest and beat the bones.

The boys drew closer and closer to each other, banging all the while. They drove the frightened deer in the woods toward the river. When the deer dashed

into the water, the men were there in
dugout canoes. They threw lassos
around the necks of the deer.

After that, the women and girls were
busy for a long time smoking the venison
and tanning the hides. Terry helped
Singing-Moon stretch and work the
leather with her hands to make it soft.

The leaves on the maple tree turned

to scarlet and gold. Then they blew away in the wind. The children gathered hickory nuts and persimmons.

The weather was much colder now. Singing-Moon made deerskin clothes for Terry and Max. They felt strange at first, especially the leather stockings and the jackets. The sleeves were not sewn on. They were separate pieces, tied onto the shoulder with laces. But the clothes were warm and soft. Before long the children were used to them.

Singing-Moon folded their T-shirts and shorts and stored them under the bench they slept on. When she finished making two pairs of moccasins, she put away their sneakers, too.

After all the harvesting and hunting was finished, the village had a festival with feasting as well as dancing. It went on for three days.

21

There wasn't much work for the two children to do now. Singing-Moon spent most of her time pounding corn into meal.

Max and Terry went to visit Wise-Defender. The women who lived in the big house with him were always preparing food, tanning hides, gathering firewood, weaving baskets, and taking care of children. They had no time to talk to the old man or listen to his stories.

Terry and Max were happy to listen to him.

Wise-Defender was carving tiny purple and white beads from two different kinds of seashells. While he worked he talked to the children.

"Everything has a spirit," he told them. "Not just people, but also animals, trees, birds, the sun, the moon, and the four winds. When an animal has to be killed, his spirit must be asked for pardon."

Wise-Defender showed them thin sticks, each about six inches long, with picture writing on them. Max and Terry couldn't read it, but Wise-Defender said that all the tribes who had dealings with the Leni-Lenape understood it. The sticks were used to send messages, and also to keep a record of history.

"Long ago the Leni-Lenape lived beside the blue sea the sun sinks into at the end of the day," Wise-Defender told them. "When trouble came, the Leni-Lenape moved to settle somewhere else. When trouble started there, they moved away again. After thousands of moons and many more moves, they came here where the sun comes up out of a gray sea. The Leni-Lenape were the first tribe to settle here.

"Other tribes say we are women, because we do not want war. But when they go to war with each other, they ask us to help make peace."

Max and Terry watched while Wise-Defender carved and polished a tiny bead.

"I've run out of shells," he said. "I was making these beads for Singing-Moon to sew on her headband."

"Where do you get the shells?" Terry asked.

"There are shell banks by the seashore," Wise-Defender told her. "Blackbird-on-the-Wing knows where they are."

He stood up and stretched. "I wonder what's going on outdoors. Let's go and see." He picked up a bow and a case of arrows. Then he pushed back the mat that covered the nearest door. Max and Terry followed him out of the house. It was getting dark.

Wise-Defender raised his bow and fitted an arrow to the cord. "Don't move!" he whispered.

Something tawny and spotted leaped from the shadows. The bowstring twanged.

A big spotted cat stumbled and fell to the ground a few feet in front of them.

"I'm sorry I have to do this to you, Old Lynx," Wise-Defender said as he shot another arrow into the cat. It took two more before the lynx was dead.

"As it gets to be winter," Wise-Defender told the children, "animals leap the fence and come close to the houses. I'd better walk you home."

22

The next day was sunny but cold and windy. "It will be colder at the shore," Blackbird-on-the-Wing told Terry. "Do you still want to go there?"

"It will be even colder soon," Terry argued. "And Wise-Defender can't make the beads for Singing-Moon's headband if he hasn't any shells."

"Wrap yourselves in these. They'll keep you warm." Singing-Moon brought three furry robes out of storage.

Max took one with shaggy black fur.

"Be sure to wear the fur on the inside," Singing-Moon said. "It's warmer that way."

All three carried their big sacks. Blackbird-on-the-Wing had a spear as well. They followed the trail along the stream, across the wide plain, and past the pond where they had gone swimming. After a while they heard seabirds screaming. The path led to a cliff. They looked down at the waters of an enormous bay.

Blackbird-on-the-Wing pointed across the water. "Those are the Haunted Woods."

"Terry," Max whispered. "I'm sure that's Staten Island!"

"Only there's no bridge," Terry agreed, "or any buildings."

The path snaked its way down the steep cliff. They had to grab hold of bushes to keep from sliding.

At the bottom of the cliff they came to a narrow, stony beach. Blackbird-on-the-Wing led them under overhanging rocks and around uprooted trees to a little cave hidden by trailing vines.

The floor of the cave was damp and covered with shells.

Blackbird-on-the-Wing showed them the two kinds of shells to gather. There were many of them there.

"We have to work fast. When the tide is in, this cave is full of water." Blackbird-on-the-Wing was using his spear to dig up live clams and oysters and drop them into his sack.

Max and Terry worked as fast as they could. When the sand under their moccasins started to become squashy, Blackbird-on-the-Wing picked up his sack and led the way out of the cave.

They walked quickly back to the path and climbed carefully up the cliff.

The wind was blowing harder now. It was much colder here than in the cave.

Terry was glad to have the soft beaver robe. It didn't look at all like her Aunt Sophie's beaver coat. That was sheared to look like velvet. And her aunt didn't wear the fur on the inside next to her skin.

Blackbird-on-the-Wing opened his bag of cornmeal. They each took a handful and chewed it slowly as they walked home with the heavy sacks.

23

Very early one morning, Max and Blackbird-on-the-Wing found a fat bear in the deadfall.

Two young men helped them drag it back to the village. Their wives joined Singing-Moon in the job of skinning the bear and cutting it up. This kept them busy for days.

The meat was shared with all the families. Some of it was skewered on sticks and held over the fire to cook. And some was placed in the coals to roast. And of course, every big wooden bowl in the village was boiling.

After the meat in one enormous bowl was cooked, Singing-Moon skimmed the fat off the top of the boiling water. She poured the fat into a clay jar. "We're lucky that bear hadn't gone to sleep for the winter. I thought I was going to run out of bear grease."

"What do you use it for?" Terry asked.

"It keeps mosquitoes away," Singing-Moon told her. "If you rub it on yourself when you're outdoors in very cold weather, it helps you stay warm. And the men use it on their hair."

The young men and boys shaved the sides of their heads and left a wide strip of hair in the middle. Now Terry knew how they made the hair stick up straight like a rooster's comb.

As the days grew shorter and colder, Singing-Moon did most of her work indoors. One day, after the meat was smoked and stored away, Terry helped her tan the bearskin. They hung it over the fire so the smoke would keep it from molding.

Singing-Moon began to feed her baby. Max pushed back the flap and came rushing through one of the doors. Blackbird-on-the-Wing was right behind him. They were both excited.

97

"A messenger has come from one of the tribes up the river," Blackbird-on-the-Wing said. "The chief of the tribe in the next valley wants to make war on his tribe. The messenger asked Wise-Defender to go back with him to make peace." Blackbird-on-the-Wing looked at Max. "Tell them the rest."

"Wise-Defender wants me to go with him," Max said.

Terry grabbed his arm. "You can't go without me!"

Max grinned. "I told Wise-Defender that's what you'd say."

"Why can't someone else go with Wise-Defender?" Singing-Moon wanted to know.

"I asked him," Blackbird-on-the-Wing told her. "Wise-Defender wouldn't tell me the reason."

24

Red-Arrow stood in front of Wise-Defender's house. He was a tall, strong young man, dressed in deerskins like the Leni-Lenape, but his face and hands were covered with designs of red paint.

"Oh, isn't he beautiful?" Snow-Flower whispered.

Everybody in the village had gathered around to look at the messenger from upriver. They all thought he looked wonderful.

"I bring you greetings of peace and friendship," Red-Arrow told them. "Your chief, Wise-Defender, has agreed to go with me to make peace with a tribe that talks of war against my people."

"I will leave tomorrow," Wise-

Defender said. "Max and Terry will come with me."

They didn't pack much for the trip. Singing-Moon gave the children each a supply of cornmeal in a little bag. She handed Terry a small flat stick and a little wooden bowl of red clay. "Be sure you paint red designs on Wise-Defender before he meets the other chiefs."

They put extra fur robes in their big sacks. Before they left, Wise-Defender gave Terry and Max each three round paddles that had wooden rims around a mesh of thin leather strips. "Keep these in your sacks."

"They look like tennis rackets," Max told his sister. "He must be planning a friendly game with the other chiefs."

The sky was clear and blue as the four travelers started on their journey. There was no wind, but the air was cold, and the ground was crunchy under their feet.

They walked along the path near the stream.

Red-Arrow went first. A stone axe hung from his belt. He carried a sack as well as a bow and arrows. Terry and Max came after him with their sacks and Max's slingshot. Wise-Defender was last, holding a sack and carrying his spear over his shoulder.

They went the same way that Blackbird-on-the-Wing had taken Terry and Max to look for seashells.

At the foot of the winding path down the cliff, Red-Arrow ran to a clump of bushes. He peeked into a thick tangle of vines and branches. "It's still here! I was

afraid someone might find it. My father and I worked for three years to make this canoe." He started to pull off the twisted vines.

The canoe was carved from a single tree and was very heavy. It took all four of them to shove it across the narrow beach into the water.

"How did you get it out of the water all by yourself?" Terry asked Red-Arrow.

"It was high tide then," he told her. "I paddled right up to the bushes and tied up the canoe. After that I covered it with vines and pine branches."

They took off their leather stockings and their moccasins and put them into their sacks. Then they waded to the boat with the sacks.

The paddles were in the canoe. Red-Arrow handed one to each of them and started paddling north across the bay.

25

It was much colder in the canoe than in the woods. Wise-Defender made them all put fur robes over their bare legs and feet. The paddling kept their arms warm.

They paddled steadily north and past a few small islands. After a while the bay split into two rivers. Red-Arrow steered the canoe up the river on the left.

Dark forests were on both sides of them. Farther on, gigantic stone cliffs rose up on one side of the river.

Still they went on paddling.

The sun was low in the sky when Red-Arrow steered the canoe to a shallow little cove by the shore. "There's a shelter here that I use when I'm on fishing trips."

They all climbed out and shoved the canoe into the weeds on the riverbank. Red-Arrow put large rocks around it to keep the canoe in place. They took their packs to an overhanging rock.

This was the shelter.

It was getting dark. Everybody chewed cornmeal and drank the clear water of the river. They made a pile of leaves and soft branches. Then they rolled themselves in their fur robes, lay down on the pile, and slept until the morning sun woke them.

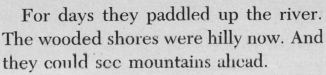

For days they paddled up the river. The wooded shores were hilly now. And they could see mountains ahead.

Each night they slept in a different shelter that Red-Arrow knew. Some were huts of branches covered with leaves. One was a small cave in a cliff.

It started raining hard on the fourth day. Wise-Defender took from his sack a beautiful cape of turkey feathers knitted together to make a smooth, downy waterproof covering. They all huddled under the big cape until the rain stopped.

Wise-Defender was afraid the tribes would start fighting before he could stop them. He was in too much of a hurry to take time to hunt or fish or cook. All they ate was cornmeal.

After dark on the seventh day, Red-Arrow paddled to the shore of the river. "My village is near here," he said. "I hoped we'd reach it before sunset, but the moon is rising, so we'll be able to follow the trail to my home."

In the dim light Red-Arrow found the clump of reeds where he always hid his canoe. They picked up their sacks and waded ashore.

Red-Arrow led them on a trail that went up a tree-covered hill.

Before they reached the top of the hill, they heard voices.

Red-Arrow signed to them to be quiet. He put his hand to his ear and listened. Then he turned and silently led them back down to the river again.

"We'll have to go to my home by the secret way," Red Arrow whispered. "Those are not my people up there in the woods. I heard them planning to attack our village tonight!"

26

The four of them made their way in a wide circle through the forest at the base of the hill. They came to the gate of a high stockade fence. It was closed and barred.

Red-Arrow hooted four times like an owl. He waited a moment and hooted once more.

A man with a spear opened the gate a crack. He looked hard at Red-Arrow in the moonlight. When he was sure who it was, he opened the gate. After they were all inside, he shut and barred it again.

Max and Terry expected to see a group of houses inside the stockade. Instead, there was just one very long house. It had a curved roof with an opening all the way along the top for smoke to come out.

The house had a single door in the center of a long wall. Red-Arrow opened it for them to go in.

Terry whispered to Wise-Defender, "Singing-Moon told me to paint you."

Wise-Defender spoke to Red-Arrow. "While you tell White-Otter I am here, I want to be alone with Terry and Max."

They stepped into the house. Many families lived here. Each one had its own fire and its own living space. The spaces were divided by mats or by animal skins. And over each fire hung meat, fish, corn, and anything else that needed to be smoked.

Red-Arrow took them to a corner of one of the spaces. It was divided from the rest of the apartment by hanging animal skins. "I am not married, so I live with my cousins. This is where I sleep. No one will bother you here. I'll come for you after I talk with Chief White-Otter."

After Red-Arrow left them, Terry took out the little wooden bowl of red clay. Wise-Defender helped her mix it with a little water from the jar near the family cooking fire.

Terry loved to draw. She used the little stick Singing-Moon had given her

to draw a red dove of peace on Wise-Defender's forehead and on the backs of his hands. She drew a sun with rays coming out of it on each of his cheeks. Then she scattered butterflies and stars all over his arms.

Max watched her. "That's enough, Terry. Don't overdo it!"

At this point Red-Arrow returned. "White-Otter wants to talk to you."

Terry and Max followed Wise-Defender to the chief's quarters.

White-Otter was a man about forty years old. He was decorated in both red and black paint.

"You can't talk peace at this point," Wise-Defender told him. "Don't wait for Strong-Stone to attack you here. Go into the woods and take him by surprise. I will go with you. My young friends will stay here."

27

White-Otter listened while Wise-Defender whispered his plan. Then he had Red-Arrow give orders to each young man in the big house.

One by one, carrying spears and bows and arrows, they slipped out of the gate and into the surrounding forest. Red-Arrow went after them.

Terry saw that Wise-Defender was ready to follow with White-Otter. "Why are you going? You're a peacemaker. This is war!"

"I have my reasons," Wise-Defender said.

The two chiefs went out into the shadows. They were careful not to step

where the moonbeams sifted down through the trees.

"Wise-Defender had a sack with him," Max told his sister. "I wonder what's in it."

"I was so mad at him that I didn't even notice the sack. Why should I care what's in it?" Terry was almost crying.

"Did you want Wise-Defender to let those men attack the village?" Max asked.

"He came here to make peace," Terry reminded him.

"He was going to get the chiefs to talk to each other," Max said, "but Strong-Stone is not in the mood for talking."

Terry didn't answer. She felt sick just thinking about what was happening out there in the forest.

All the people in the big house were very quiet. Although nobody had told them what was going on, they seemed to feel danger.

The children lay on the benches, but they kept their eyes wide open. Every mother stayed close to her family. The old people huddled around the cooking fires. And everybody was listening.

Max was expecting whoops and hollers like the ones he'd heard in old cowboy-and-Indian movies. Terry was waiting for shrieks of pain, but all they heard was the wind in the tall pine trees.

After what seemed like years of waiting, they heard an owl hoot four times.

There was a pause. Then the owl hooted once more.

Perhaps it was a trick. The old men picked up spears. Max put a stone in his slingshot. They went out of the house to open the gate in the stockade.

When the gate was opened slightly, they heard Wise-Defender's voice. "Open wide," he commanded, "and welcome your guests! They are tired and hungry."

Both Max and Terry were sure it was a terrible trick of some kind. But the old men opened the gate wide.

The strangers walked in slowly, one at a time.

28

The strangers entered the big house. They were carrying their weapons, and they held their heads high, but they wouldn't look anybody in the eye. The last to come in was their chief, Strong-Stone, walking between Wise-Defender and White-Otter.

Strong-Stone was painted all over in fierce designs of black and red. He, too, held his head high, but he glared at everybody.

The women in the house were soon busy heating stones to boil their vegetables and cornmeal and putting chunks of meat to cook over the blazing coals. As soon as any food was ready, the guests were served.

At first they seemed shy about eating, but once they started, the strangers began to smile and talk to the women who were serving them. After he'd finished a large serving of roast beaver-tail, even Strong-Stone stopped glaring.

When all the people in the house had eaten their fill, the floor was spread with soft skins for the guests to sleep on. Before long they lay down beside their bows and arrows and went to sleep.

Max and Terry shared Red-Arrow's corner of his cousins' apartment with him and Wise-Defender. They fell asleep as soon as they lay down.

Early next morning, Wise-Defender whispered in Terry's ear, "Wake up!"

Terry opened her eyes and sat up.

Still whispering, Wise-Defender said, "You must fill a large bowl with water and get it so hot that it steams. Don't let anybody drop any food into it. I want you and Max to wash your hair, your face, and any skin that's not hidden by your clothes. Try not to let anyone see you doing this. Stay here until I send for you." Wise-Defender walked away.

Max and Red-Arrow were still sleeping. Everyone else in the house was fast asleep, too.

Terry saw that a few embers were glowing in last night's cooking fire. She added sticks and dry grass from a pile and blew on the red embers until they burst into flame. Then she pushed stones into the fire and threw bigger logs onto it.

She set a big wooden bowl near the fire and filled it from a container of water. When the water began to steam, Terry held her hands over it until they were damp. She rubbed the dirt off them. Then she leaned over the bowl

and let the steam drift over her face and her hair. She had to keep adding stones to the bowl to keep it boiling. She rubbed and steamed as much of herself as she could. She didn't have a mirror, so she decided to wake Max.

Terry put her finger on Max's lips.

He opened his eyes.

"*Sh-sh!* Just tell me if I've got all the dirt off myself," Terry said.

It was all Max could do to keep from yelling, but he managed to whisper. "Are you nuts?"

"Wise-Defender told me to get washed," Terry explained. "He wants you to get cleaned up, too. I guess he's ashamed of us. We are pretty dirty."

29

Most of the day Wise-Defender was in a meeting with White-Otter and Strong-Stone. They sat around the fire in White-Otter's living space. They talked in loud, angry voices. Everybody else in the big house was very quiet. They were listening to what the chiefs had to say.

Terry and Max stayed in Red-Arrow's corner of his cousin's apartment. They were now both as clean as they could get without soap. Terry stared at her brother. "I'd forgotten how blond your hair is."

Max laughed. "You should see yourself. You're pink! And that makes your eyes greener."

They stopped talking to listen to the chiefs. They wanted to know what had happened in the woods the night before to stop Strong-Stone's attack.

Nobody spoke of that. Instead the two chiefs argued about hunting and fishing territories, about planting fields and berry patches. They seemed to say the same things over and over.

Sometimes Wise-Defender would suggest something. Neither of the chiefs wanted to listen to him.

Wise-Defender left them and went to where Max and Terry were waiting for him. "Come with me," he said.

He led them to where the two chiefs were still arguing. Wise-Defender held up his hand. "Stop! I want you to meet these messengers who came to save you from the horrors of war."

The chiefs were seated on the ground

by the fire. They took one look at the children standing over them and then seemed even more terrified than Singing-Moon when she first saw them.

Terry had acted in a school play about Greek gods. "Foolish mortals," she growled in a deep voice. "Listen to your

wise friend, before disaster strikes!"

Max folded his arms and looked stern.

Wise-Defender kneeled before the children. "Have mercy! Do not destroy these good men. Give them a chance to learn to share the gifts of nature."

Terry was having so much fun that she would have gone on talking, but Max dragged his sister away.

Wise-Defender sat on the ground facing the two chiefs and suggested that they should go fishing on different days. Strong-Stone said he'd fish on the first day after the full moon. White-Otter liked the second day. Before long they found ways to solve all their problems.

Wise-Defender brought out a clay

pipe with a copper bowl. The two leaders smoked the Pipe of Peace together.

Terry and Max went back to find Red-Arrow in his cousins' living quarters.

"Please tell us what happened last night," Terry begged.

Red-Arrow grinned. "Wise-Defender took along a sackful of ropes. Each time one of our men surprised one of theirs and aimed a spear or an arrow at him, another one of our men would lasso, gag, and tie him up. Then Wise-Defender told him all we wanted was a peace talk. If he promised to come peacefully, we would let him keep his weapons and give him food and shelter.

"I don't know how he did it, but Wise-Defender got every one, even their chief, to agree to his terms."

Red-Arrow took a good look at Max and Terry. "You look different," he said. "If I didn't know you, I'd be scared."

30

Paddling down the river was much quicker than paddling up had been. The canoe followed the current. It rained on the third day. After sunset the rain turned to snow. In the morning the sky was clear, but the air was colder.

Very early on the fifth day, Red-Arrow steered into the wide bay.

Max jumped from the boat onto the narrow beach, carrying his sack. He helped Wise-Defender get ashore with his things. Then Terry threw her sack onto the beach and leaped after it.

Red-Arrow wanted to be home before the river froze. He waved good-bye. The others started up the cliff. It had been snowing, and the path was hard to find.

At the top, the snow on the level ground was much deeper. It reached to Terry's knees. Her sack was dragging.

Wise-Defender opened it and pulled out the three paddles she had been lugging, and then took the three others from Max's pack. Terry stood on one foot at a time and leaned on Max while Wise-Defender tied paddles to her ankles with wide strips of rawhide.

Max saw that they were snowshoes. He helped Wise-Defender tie a pair on himself, and then Wise-Defender helped Max.

The sacks were lighter now, and the three of them could walk across the

snow as if it were a carpet. They followed the path to the Leni-Lenape village. Singing-Moon and Blackbird-on-the-Wing were so happy to see them that they ran to tell the news to everyone.

The big drum started to beat. The people danced till the snow was pounded flat. They were still singing when Max and Terry fell asleep.

When Max woke, he caught sight of his sneakers, T-shirt, and shorts under the bench he had been sleeping on.

Suddenly Max felt like putting on his old clothes. After he was dressed, he shook his sister. Terry sat up and stared at him.

"Why are you wearing your shorts?" she asked.

"I don't know," Max said. "I was just thinking about the sweat lodge. This would be a good time to explore it. Everyone's asleep."

Max handed Terry her old clothes. "Put these on. We won't need our deerskin clothing now."

Terry changed into her shirt, shorts, and red sneakers. She followed Max out of the little house and through the sleeping village to the sweat lodge. Max lifted the dome off the hole and went after Terry down a set of steps to the lodge below.

No steaming leaves were here now. The clay floor was swept clean. The ceiling was too low for them to stand, and somehow they couldn't find the steps they had come in by.

There must be another entrance to the lodge. They made their way toward a faint green glow, which seemed to be at the end of a long tunnel.

At last Terry and Max crawled out into bright sunshine. They turned to look at the tunnel, but it was gone.

They were in their own yard. The back door of the house opened. Their mother and father came out.

Mr. Robertson looked at Max and Terry. "Your mother was worried about leaving you alone, but I see we weren't gone long enough for you kids to get into trouble."

"Your dad changed his mind about building a wall when he found out how much it would cost," Mrs. Robertson told them.

"I'm going to build a stockade fence instead," Mr. Robertson said.